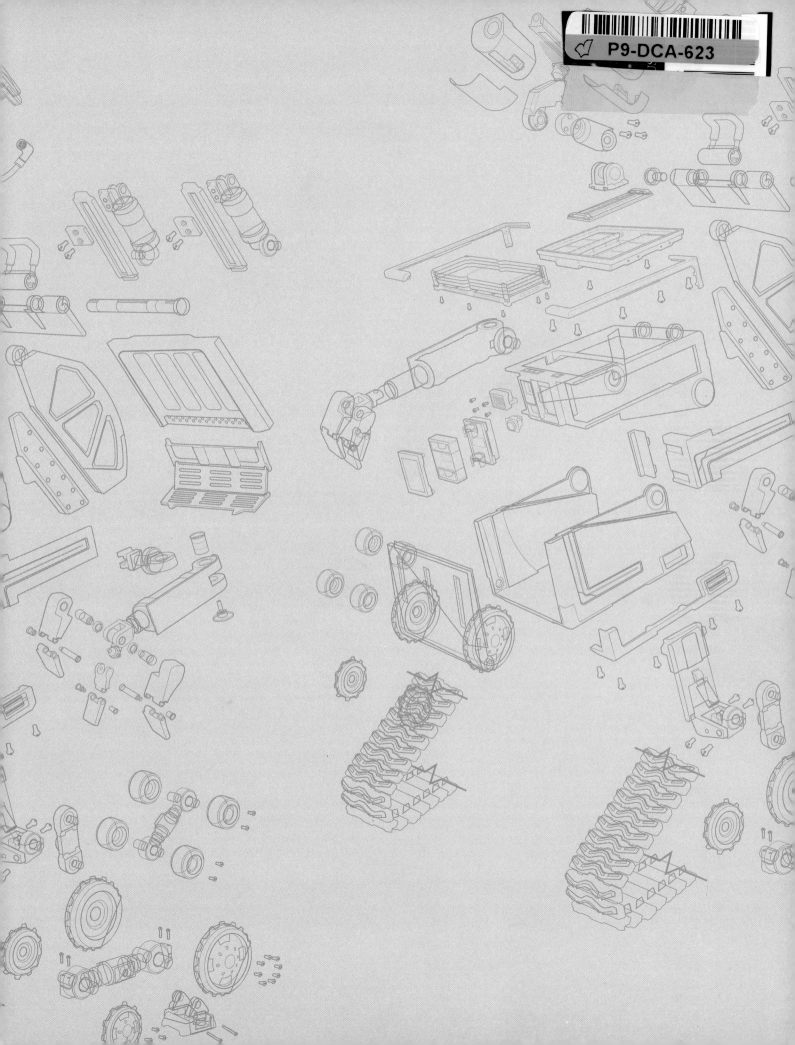

DISNEY · PIXAR

WALL·E

THE INTERGALACTIC GUIDE

WALL·E

Written by Catherine Saunders

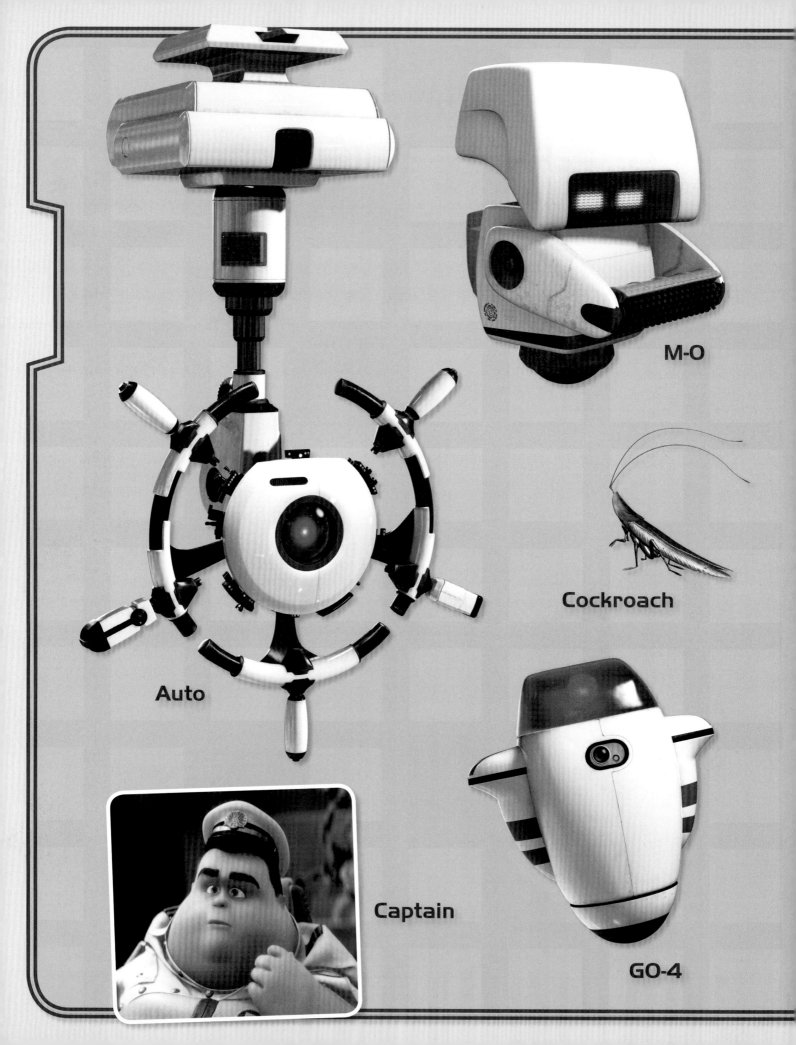

Auto

M-O

Cockroach

Captain

GO-4

DISNEY · PIXAR

WALL·E

THE INTERGALACTIC GUIDE

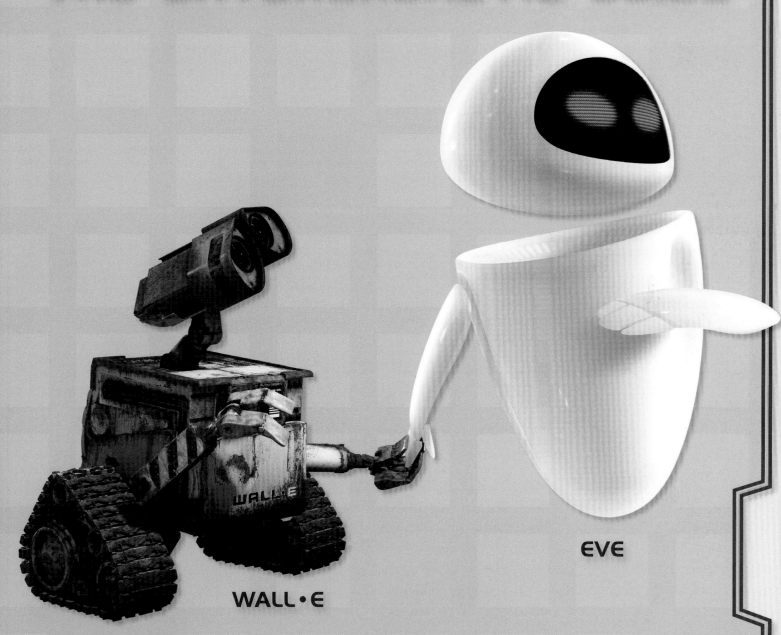

EVE

WALL·E

Written by Catherine Saunders

CONTENTS

INTRODUCTION

Have you ever wondered what life will be like in the future? How will humans be living eight hundred years from now? Well, you are about to find out—and it's not a pretty sight!

It's the year 2805! Earth is a giant trash pile and humans have moved to outer space. For seven hundred years they have been orbiting the Earth in luxury spaceships while back on Earth, a group of waste control robots have been left with a massive clean-up job. However, one by one the robots have worn out, until now only one robot is left.

EARTH

This is how Earth looks in the year 2805. With all the people long gone, it is a quiet and lonely wasteland. The streets are deserted, except for huge piles of trash, and even the clean-up robots have long since stopped working and turned to rust. Could this be the end of the line for planet Earth?

BnL

All around are the remains of the Buy n Large Corporation—the company that organized all aspects of life on Earth, including the evacuation to space in 2105.

Trash Central

Earth lies in ruins and is piled high with trash created by humans.

The Plan
When humans left Earth, it was supposed to be temporary. BnL promised a global clean-up and a good-as-new Earth for humans to come home to. However, things haven't quite worked out that way.

Trash Hero
Wait a minute! Earth is not completely deserted. One brave little robot has survived.

WALL•E

When humans abandoned Earth, the BnL Corporation left behind thousands of robot units to start the clean-up operation. Gradually all the robots broke down, except for one. Meet Waste Allocation Load Lifter, Earth class—or WALL•E for short. He may be a little rusty, but he's a special guy!

WALL•E's eyes work like binoculars—he can adjust their focus to magnify objects that are far away.

Battery and control panel.

Triangular-shaped treads help WALL•E move around on the trash-covered terrain.

WALL•E's body is hollow to allow him to take in trash and turn it into perfect cubes.

SOLAR CHARGE LEVEL

WALL•E

WALL•E is an unusual robot. He is full of curiosity and loves finding strange and wonderful treasures amongst the trash.

DID YOU KNOW?

WALL•E is great at cubing trash but when he is scared he can also turn himself into a cube! Retreating inside his hollow body is the perfect way to hide from danger. WALL•E also uses his cube mode when he shuts down at night.

Versatile robot "hands" can be used in a variety of ways to lift and sort trash.

These buttons are located just above WALL•E's control panel and allow him to play cheerful music while he works.

Rusty Hero
WALL•E doesn't know why he is the only robot to survive so he just gets on with his job. In fact, his broken comrades are a useful source of spare parts for this resourceful little robot!

WALL•E's only companion is a cockroach and the insect is a surprisingly loyal friend. Fortunately, he's also tough—which comes in handy when his pal WALL•E accidentally runs him over!

WALL•E is solar powered, which makes him a very environmentally friendly robot. When he wants to re-charge his battery, all WALL•E needs is sunshine.

A DAY'S WORK

All day, every day, WALL•E busily collects, compacts, cubes, and stacks trash. It might not be everyone's idea of the perfect job, but WALL•E seems happy enough. Despite being the last robot left on Earth, he works hard to clear up the trash and never complains.

At first glance, you might think this is the skyline of a major city. Take a closer look—some of those tall buildings are actually towers of trash!

Collecting trash has its interesting moments, such as finding this tiny green plant. WALL•E has no idea what it is, but his instincts tell him that he must treat it with care.

WALL•E

WORKING TO DIG YOU OUT!

Once upon a time there was a whole fleet of WALL•E robots cleaning up Earth, but all but one have long since retired to the eternal junkyard.

Soon WALL•E will have made another giant tower of trash!

WALL•E raises his extendable legs to reach the top of the trash pile.

Executive Robot
It might look like a rusty briefcase, but WALL•E keeps his treasured possessions, including the precious plant, inside an old cooler.

WALL•E patiently stacks the cubes of trash.

WALL•E's mechanical arms are designed to gather and organize trash.

Cleaning Up
First, WALL•E scoops the trash into his hollow middle. Then, he compacts it and spits out a small cube. WALL•E then neatly stacks the trash cube and starts all over again.

WALL•E's home was originally used by the Buy n Large Corporation to transport and store their clean-up robots. Now that WALL•E is the only robot left on Earth, he has made it into a comfortable and stylish robot residence.

WALL•E arrives home after cleaning up trash all day.

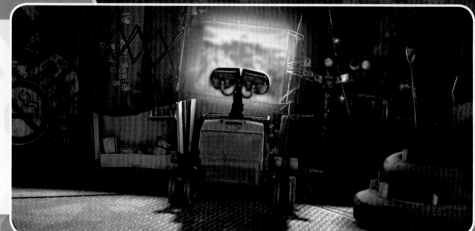

WALL•E is an old romantic. He adores watching old movies on his video player. His favorites are musicals from the mid-20th century. He can't quite understand what it means when couples in love hold hands, but he has a feeling it's important.

HOME SWEET HOME

It's rusty on the outside but inside it has everything WALL·E needs.

After a busy day of sorting trash, WALL·E motors home. For the rusty robot, home is a broken-down BnL Corporation truck. It is situated by the side of a derelict freeway and although it might not look like a palace, for WALL·E it is a place where he can truly be himself.

Bachelor Pad

WALL·E's home may be a little rusty on the outside (like its owner) but inside it is the perfect place for the hardworking robot to relax.

WALL·E's truck is perched high on an abandoned freeway, which gives him a great view of the deserted city. If only he had someone to share it with!

WALL·E can't really say what he likes about the curious objects he finds in the trash, and he certainly doesn't know how they work. He just likes collecting things.

The thought of going home and hanging up his treads keeps WALL·E going while he is hard at work.

Danger!
One day, something unusual happens: WALL•E notices a tiny red dot in front of his trailer home. It seems to be coming from the sky!

Soon, one dot becomes a circle of bright red dots that seem to be closing in on WALL•E. The scared robot must act fast!

Every day WALL•E's life follows the same pattern—he works hard cleaning up trash and then goes home and watches his favorite movie. Although WALL•E is content, deep down he senses that there is more to life than being alone. One day, a visitor arrives on Earth and ends up taking WALL•E on an unexpected adventure.

Suddenly the red dots disappear and WALL•E is engulfed by a giant dust cloud!

SURPRISE VISIT

The capsule opens to finally reveal its occupant—a sleek, modern robot. WALL•E is instantly smitten with the beautiful visitor, but it soon becomes clear that she has other things on her mind.

From a portal on the underside of the spaceship a long, thin chute emerges and a capsule is lowered to the ground.

WALL•E retreats into cube mode and watches in amazement as a strange spaceship lands on Earth.

WALL•E follows the new arrival as she travels around. He watches as she scans various objects. What is she looking for?

As WALL•E adoringly observes the beautiful robot, it becomes clear that she hasn't found what she is looking for. WALL•E takes the opportunity to introduce himself.

WALL•E's visitor is a probe-bot who has been sent to Earth to check for signs of plant life. The Extra-terrestrial Vegetation Evaluator, otherwise known as EVE, takes her mission very seriously. At first she doesn't even notice the rusty robot following her as she searches Earth.

EVE's big, blue eyes convey a variety of expressons.

EVE is just one of many probe-bots sent to Earth to scan for signs of plant life. The probe-bots may all look identical but EVE is special, at least that's what WALL•E thinks.

This arm hides a secret weapon!

EVE's control panel is located in the center of her chest.

EVE moves with speed, grace, and purpose. She hovers above the ground when she is searching for vegetation.

EVE is certainly no damsel in distress. Her right arm conceals a powerful laser cannon which can blast rocks and space ships into smithereens!

A smitten WALL•E tries to win EVE's heart by making a statue of her out of trash! She is not impressed.

EVE uses the powerful laser in her chest to scan and evaluate objects she finds on Earth. As soon as she finds what she is looking for, her mission will be complete.

Pristine Droid
Sleek, clean, shiny, and elegant, EVE is the complete opposite of the cute, but rusty WALL•E. She is smart, focused, and determined to complete her mission. WALL•E thinks she is simply wonderful!

EVE's arms function like wings to help her move about.

19

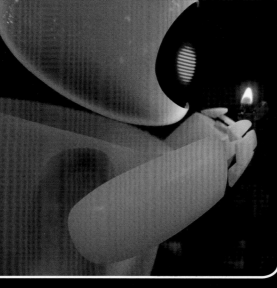

When WALL•E finds this bra he has no idea what it is, in fact he concludes it must be some kind of sunshade for the eyes!

EVE is a little smarter than WALL•E when it comes to working out what his treasures are for. But when it comes to love, WALL•E is way ahead of EVE.

When WALL•E finds a diamond ring, he is much more interested in its box.

Mission Complete
When WALL•E shows EVE his plant, EVE's sensors go into overdrive. She has found what she is looking for! EVE takes the plant and stores it in a compartment in her chest. Her mission to Earth is over, so EVE shuts down and waits to be transported back to space.

Bits and Bobs
WALL•E's collection of weird and wonderful knick knacks may not be worth a lot of money but they are all he has. Besides, what use is money when you are the only robot left on Earth?

WALL•E uses his cooler to transport his treasures home.

Birdcage

Bowling pin

Rubber ducks

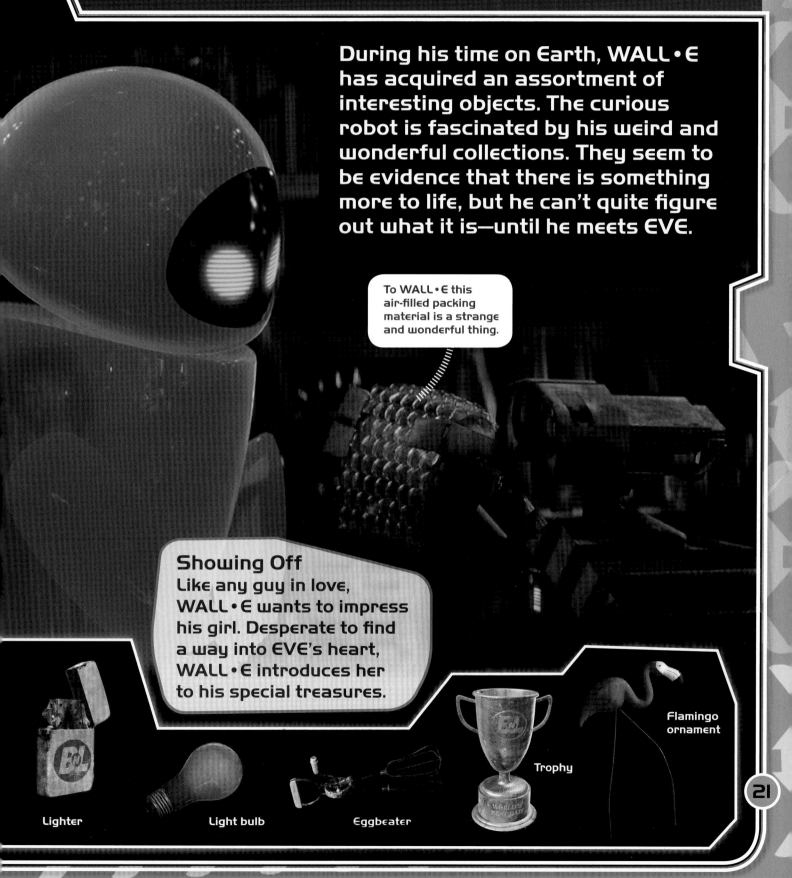

During his time on Earth, WALL•E has acquired an assortment of interesting objects. The curious robot is fascinated by his weird and wonderful collections. They seem to be evidence that there is something more to life, but he can't quite figure out what it is—until he meets EVE.

To WALL•E this air-filled packing material is a strange and wonderful thing.

Showing Off
Like any guy in love, WALL•E wants to impress his girl. Desperate to find a way into EVE's heart, WALL•E introduces her to his special treasures.

Lighter

Light bulb

Eggbeater

Trophy

Flamingo ornament

21

LOVESICK ROBOT

EVE likes WALL•E—he is sweet and he makes her giggle, but she is too focused on her mission to find time for romance. When she discovers the plant amongst WALL•E's knick knacks, EVE's mission is complete and she goes into sleep mode. Poor WALL•E has no idea what has happened and tries desperately to revive the robot he loves.

WALL•E gazes adoringly at the unconscious EVE.

WALL•E clasps his hands together in a bashful pose.

The Power of Love
First WALL•E puts EVE in his charging spot on top of his truck, hoping the sun will revive her. But unlike WALL•E, EVE is not solar powered.

True Gentleman
While EVE stands motionless on the roof of WALL•E's truck, a thunderstorm approaches. Like the romantic heroes in his favorite movies, WALL•E tries to protect his leading lady.

Unfortunately, poor WALL•E gets struck by lightning. Twice!

WALL•E uses a string of Christmas lights as a leash to pull EVE along.

The green light that flickers on EVE's chest indicates that she has the plant and her mission has been a success.

Heart to Heart

A desperate WALL•E tries to jump-start EVE by connecting a power cable from his heart battery to EVE's. Unfortunately, WALL•E triggers EVE's automatic defense system and receives a massive electric shock!

Robot Romance

WALL•E 's idea of what it means to be in love comes from the old movies he watches over and over again on videotape. So, the rusty romeo sets out to awaken EVE with a mixture of robot intelligence and good old fashioned romance!

In a spontaneous romantic gesture, WALL•E uses his laser to burn his name and EVE's into the side of a trash can.

Watching the Sunset

In desperation, WALL•E uses his last resort—romance. He takes EVE to watch the sunset and hopes that the beauty of the view will wake her up.

23

WALL•E can't believe his eyes. His beloved EVE is being taken away from him. He must save her!

EVE's spaceship has been sent to collect all the probe-bots and return them to space. Only EVE has a flashing green light.

WALL•E sees some amazing sights up in space. He flies past the moon, has a quick re-charge near the sun, and marvels at the twinkling stars.

Despite WALL•E's best efforts, EVE remains in sleep mode. WALL•E doesn't know what else to try, when suddenly EVE's spaceship returns. WALL•E watches in horror as his beloved EVE is carried away. Ordering his loyal cockroach pal to "stay!" WALL•E leaps into action and follows his heart.

THRILL RIDE

Following his Heart
WALL•E races after EVE and launches himself at her departing spaceship. Holding on tight, he begins the ride of his life.

As the spaceship leaves Earth's atmosphere, it bursts through a field of disused BnL satellites. Once in space, the ship's boosters shut down and WALL•E can enjoy the ride.

WALL•E clings onto the side of EVE's spaceship for a fast ride through the galaxy!

A Long Way From Home
WALL•E's mission to save EVE has taken him billions of miles away from Earth. However, the lovesick robot doesn't feel scared—all he cares about is rescuing EVE.

Hover transporters like this are a popular mode of transport in the year 2805.

Successful Mission
One by one the robots are scanned and when it is EVE's turn, the scan reveals that she has found vegetation on Earth. As an alarm goes off, EVE is quickly loaded onto a hover transporter.

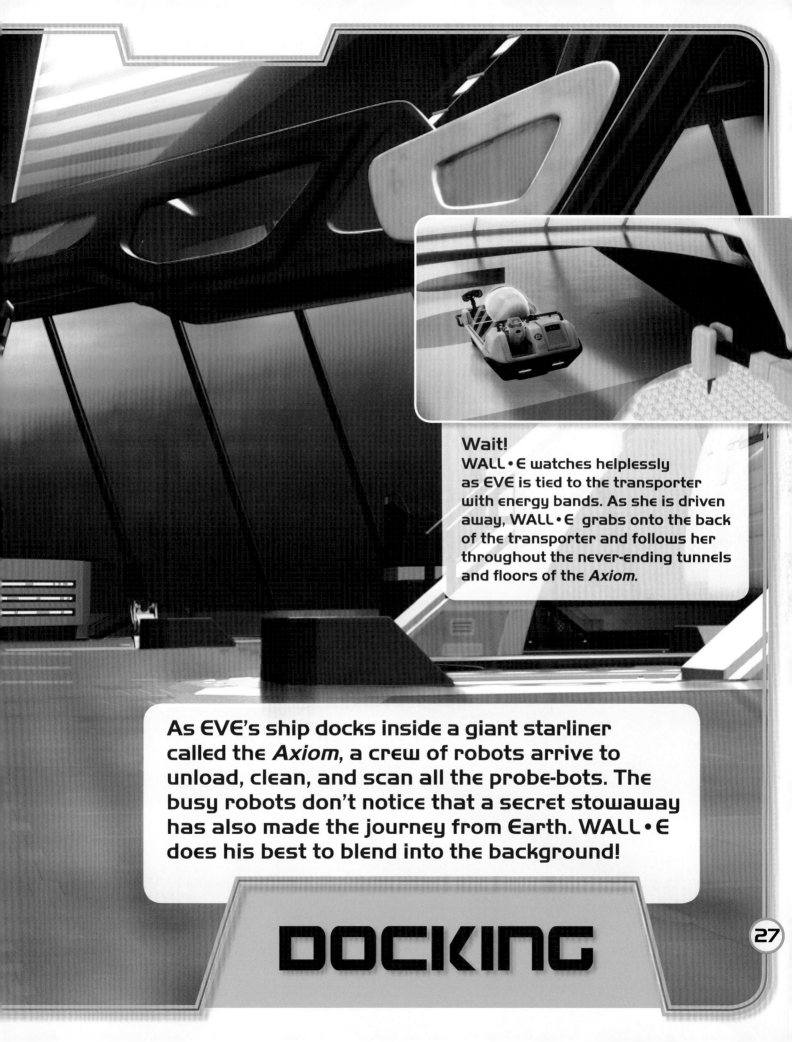

Wait!
WALL•E watches helplessly as EVE is tied to the transporter with energy bands. As she is driven away, WALL•E grabs onto the back of the transporter and follows her throughout the never-ending tunnels and floors of the *Axiom*.

As EVE's ship docks inside a giant starliner called the *Axiom*, a crew of robots arrive to unload, clean, and scan all the probe-bots. The busy robots don't notice that a secret stowaway has also made the journey from Earth. WALL•E does his best to blend into the background!

DOCKING

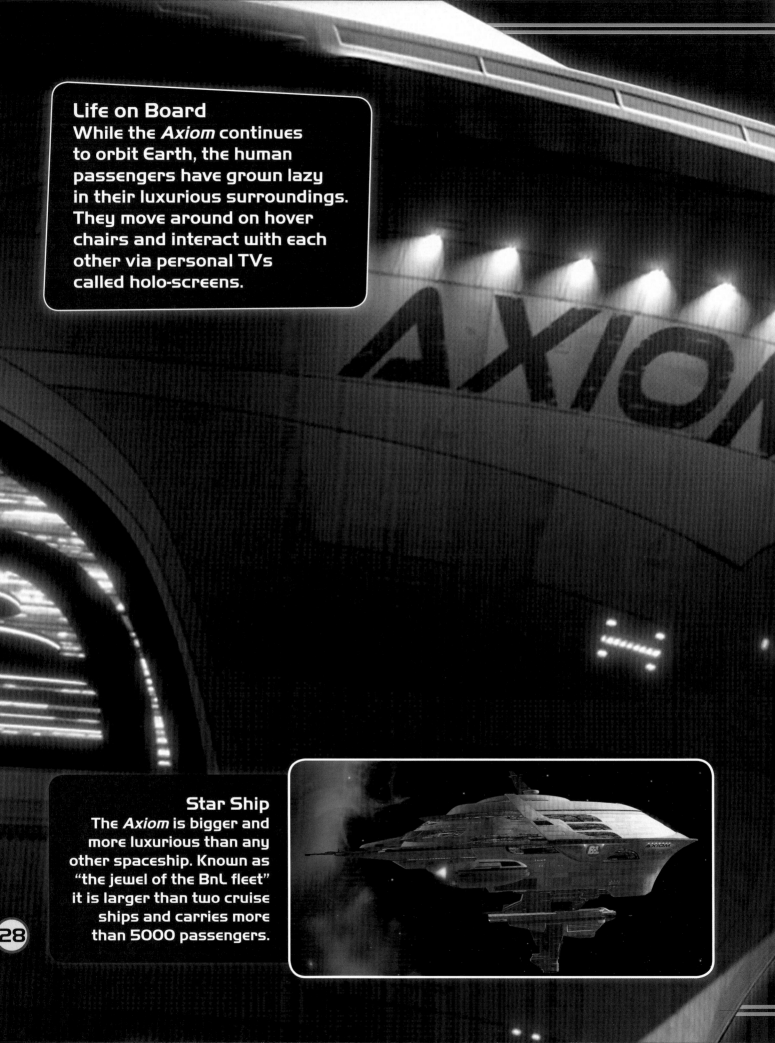

Life on Board

While the *Axiom* continues to orbit Earth, the human passengers have grown lazy in their luxurious surroundings. They move around on hover chairs and interact with each other via personal TVs called holo-screens.

Star Ship

The *Axiom* is bigger and more luxurious than any other spaceship. Known as "the jewel of the BnL fleet" it is larger than two cruise ships and carries more than 5000 passengers.

THE AXIOM

For the last seven hundred years humans have been orbiting the Earth in luxury spaceships. The most prestigious ship in the fleet is an executive star liner called the *Axiom*. It is commanded by a human known as the Captain with the aid of hundreds of robots.

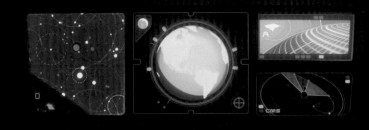

The *Axiom*'s control center is located at the top of the ship and is known as "the bridge". Although the Captain is in charge, the ship is mostly run by the sinister autopilot, Auto.

The *Axiom* is home to hundreds of robots, all with highly specialized jobs. From cleaning-bots and repair-bots to beautician-bots and nanny-bots, there's a robot to take care of all human needs.

29

THE CAPTAIN

Disappeared!
However, when the Captain opens up EVE, the plant is gone! EVE blames WALL•E, but he is not the culprit...

In 2805 humans are lazy, overweight creatures and the *Axiom*'s Captain is no exception. Until now, he has been happy to leave the running of the ship to Auto, but EVE's discovery of the plant changes everything.

Time to Change
The Captain is used to taking it easy, but he's about to be called into action—thanks to WALL•E and EVE.

WALL•E Hides
When the Captain catches sight of WALL•E, he assumes he is a reject-bot and sends him off to the repair ward.

Taking Charge
Auto brings EVE to meet the Captain. He activates a pre-recorded message from the CEO of BnL informing the baffled Captain that since vegetation has been found on Earth, humans can return home.

Hidden Agenda
Although Auto seems to be helping the Captain, he is secretly following code A113. What can it mean?

"Manuel"
The Captain consults the ship's manual to find out what do with with EVE's discovery.

CONFIRM AQUISITION

PLANT EXTRACTION

SUBCUTANEOUS CIRCUITRY

31

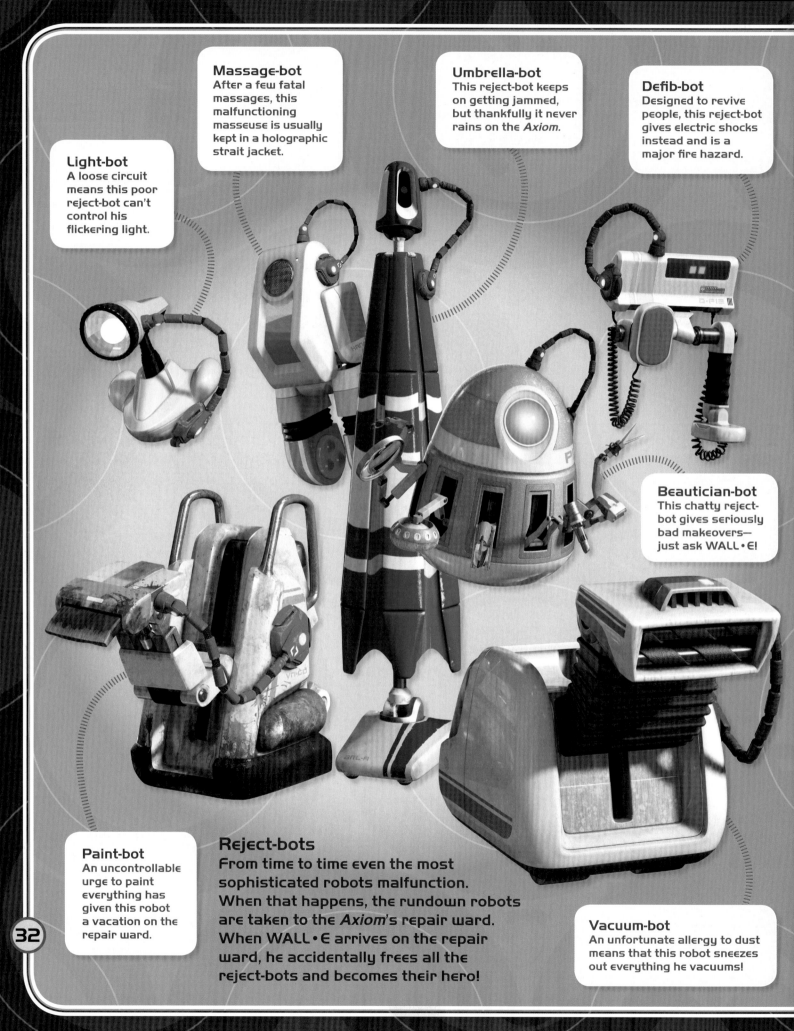

Light-bot
A loose circuit means this poor reject-bot can't control his flickering light.

Massage-bot
After a few fatal massages, this malfunctioning masseuse is usually kept in a holographic strait jacket.

Umbrella-bot
This reject-bot keeps on getting jammed, but thankfully it never rains on the *Axiom*.

Defib-bot
Designed to revive people, this reject-bot gives electric shocks instead and is a major fire hazard.

Beautician-bot
This chatty reject-bot gives seriously bad makeovers—just ask WALL•E!

Paint-bot
An uncontrollable urge to paint everything has given this robot a vacation on the repair ward.

Reject-bots
From time to time even the most sophisticated robots malfunction. When that happens, the rundown robots are taken to the *Axiom*'s repair ward. When WALL•E arrives on the repair ward, he accidentally frees all the reject-bots and becomes their hero!

Vacuum-bot
An unfortunate allergy to dust means that this robot sneezes out everything he vacuums!

ROBOTS

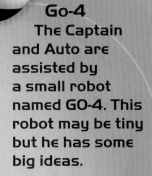

There's a robot for everything on the *Axiom*, from major jobs such as steering the spaceship to tiny tasks such as holding food cups. While humans sit about doing very little, the robots work hard day and night to ensure that life in outer space runs smoothly and efficiently.

Go-4
The Captain and Auto are assisted by a small robot named GO-4. This robot may be tiny but he has some big ideas.

Auto
Although the Captain is in charge of the *Axiom*, he lets the ship's automated steering wheel, Auto, do most of the work. However, Auto is secretly following someone else's orders.

Steward-bots
These security robots keep order on the *Axiom*. They look for signs of trouble using their camera eyes and are always ready and willing to use their freeze beams.

GO-4 helps Auto carry out his secret order, known as A113, but the Captain has no idea what these rogue robots are up to.

33

M-O has only three things on his mind: scrub, scrub, scrub!

Cleaning Machine
Microbe Obliterator, or M-O to his friends, only has one focus in life—to make his surroundings as clean as possible. But WALL•E is about to give him a seriously messy problem!

34

Super-efficient roller for cleaning and making things shine.

Deep down M-O knows that WALL•E is deliberately teasing him by leaving trails of dirt behind, but he just can't help himself—he has to clean! Just imagine what M-O would do if he ever visited Earth...

WALL•E is the filthiest thing M-O has ever seen and he is desperate to clean him. But WALL•E can't resist messing with the little guy by trying to stay just out of his reach.

M-O follows WALL•E and EVE around the *Axiom*, diligently cleaning up WALL•E's dirty tracks. It's only a matter of time before M-O gets mixed up in their crazy adventure.

Although WALL•E becomes a hero to the reject-bots when he sets them free, another little robot will also prove to be a very useful friend to WALL•E. He may be small, but the spotless M-O is an obsessive cleaning-bot who takes his job very seriously.

M-O

HOPE

After seven hundred years living in luxury in outer space humans have pretty much forgotten about Earth. With every need supplied by BnL, people have fallen into a state of extreme laziness and no longer even think of Earth as home. However, humans are about to get a wake up call, thanks to WALL•E!

Amazing Discovery
WALL•E is used to finding interesting things amongst the piles of trash, but when he spots a tiny plant he has a feeling that it's special. Little does he know that it will lead him on the adventure of a lifetime and change the future of the human race!

The Seeds of Hope
WALL•E has no idea what the plant actually is so he stores it in one of his other treasures—an old boot! Fortunately, EVE arrives a short time later to rescue the precious plant.

The plant is the first sign of new life on Earth for seven hundred years. WALL•E carefully picks it up and carries it home in his cooler.

Humans have no need for shoes in space—they don't walk anywhere!

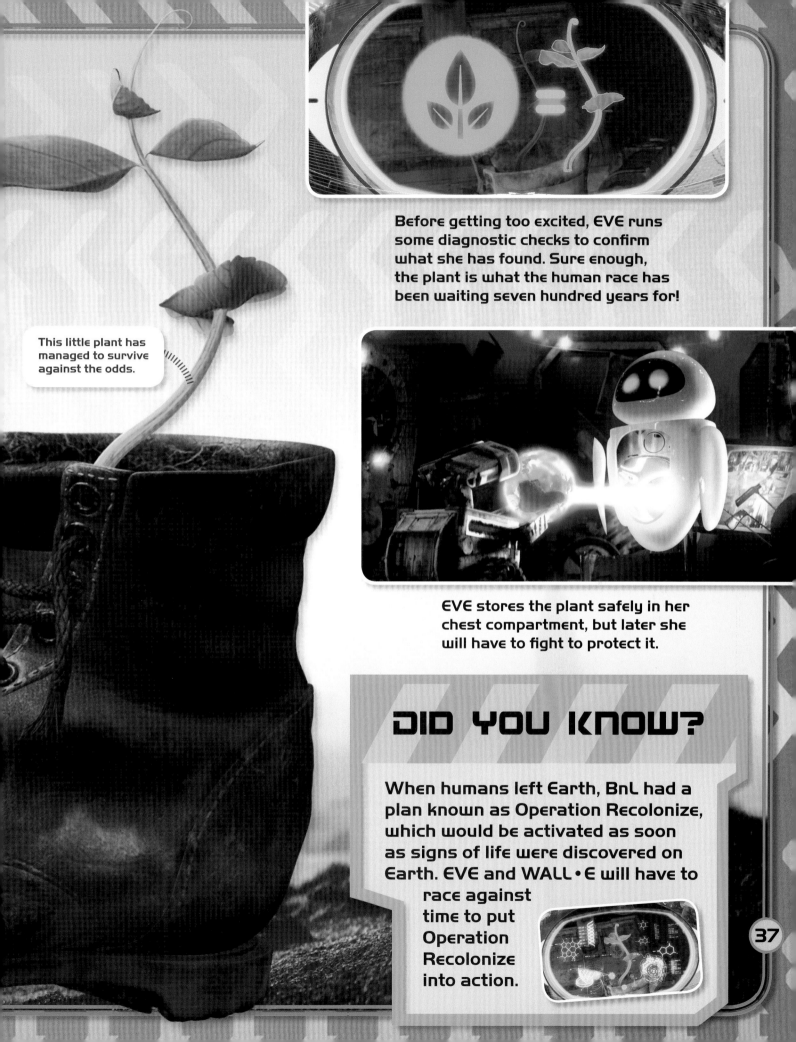

Before getting too excited, EVE runs some diagnostic checks to confirm what she has found. Sure enough, the plant is what the human race has been waiting seven hundred years for!

This little plant has managed to survive against the odds.

EVE stores the plant safely in her chest compartment, but later she will have to fight to protect it.

DID YOU KNOW?

When humans left Earth, BnL had a plan known as Operation Recolonize, which would be activated as soon as signs of life were discovered on Earth. EVE and WALL•E will have to race against time to put Operation Recolonize into action.

GREAT ESCAPE

Breakout!
When EVE is being cleaned and checked over in the repair ward, WALL•E becomes convinced that she is being hurt. He rushes to save her, but ends up pulling off her arm and setting all the reject-bots free!

WALL•E doesn't set out to be a hero, but he just can't help it. When he finds himself on the passenger level of the *Axiom*, the zoned-out humans don't even notice him. But as he searches for EVE, WALL•E inadvertently changes the lives of everyone around him. He also has a few adventures of his own along the way...

Escape Plan
EVE thinks that WALL•E is getting in the way and she just wants him off the *Axiom*. However, the devoted WALL•E will not go anywhere without her.

Rogue Robots
With the steward-bots in hot pursuit, EVE picks up WALL•E and flies away. They are public enemy #1 on the *Axiom*.

Secret Mission
WALL•E and EVE hide in the escape pod bay, just as GO-4 arrives and drops the plant into one of the escape pods. What is he up to?

Small escape pods like this one are used for emergency launches.

WALL•E has no idea where the pod is headed!

Green Fingers
WALL•E races into the escape pod to rescue the plant, just as GO-4 launches the pod into space!

Oops!
WALL•E panics and pushes all the buttons on the pod's console—including the big red self-destruct button!

Quick Thinking
Thanks to a handy fire extinguisher, WALL•E manages to escape the pod just before it explodes. As he floats in space, EVE flies out to rescue him.

39

SPACE KISS

After a few near-misses, WALL•E and EVE are finally re-united in space. WALL•E opens his chest and shows EVE that he has saved the plant. EVE is overjoyed and the happy robot spins WALL•E around in a weightless dance.

WALL•E has loved EVE since the first moment he laid eyes on her.

EVE is beginning to realize how brave and loyal WALL•E is.

True Love?
EVE is so happy to see WALL•E and the precious plant that she can't control her feelings. She gives WALL•E a thank you "kiss" and sparks fly between the romantic robots. Literally!

BUY N LARGE

BnL Railways

Back in the 22nd century, life on Earth was big business. Everything—from government to gas stations, transportation to trash control—was run by a huge and powerful corporation called Buy n Large. The CEO of BnL made all the big decisions for the human race, including evacuating everyone to outer space.

WALL•E himself is a product of the Buy n Large Corporation.

BnL Stores

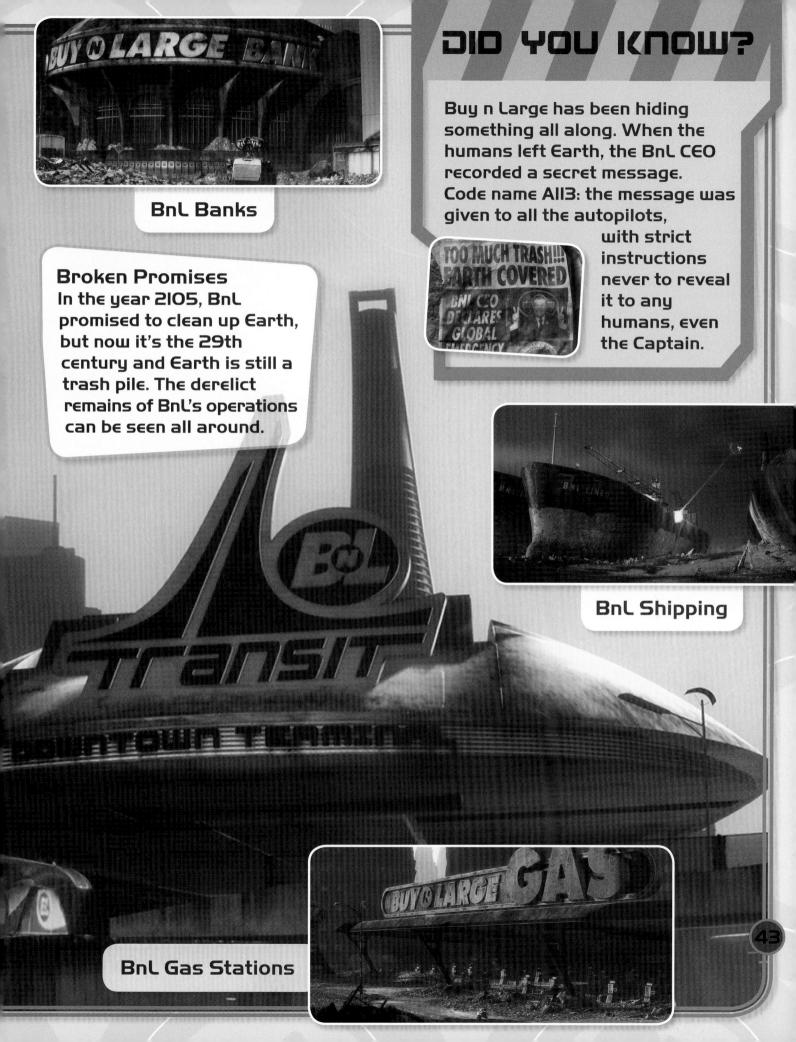

BnL Banks

Buy n Large has been hiding something all along. When the humans left Earth, the BnL CEO recorded a secret message. Code name A113: the message was given to all the autopilots, with strict instructions never to reveal it to any humans, even the Captain.

TOO MUCH TRASH!!!
EARTH COVERED
BNL CEO DECLARES GLOBAL EMERGENCY

Broken Promises
In the year 2105, BnL promised to clean up Earth, but now it's the 29th century and Earth is still a trash pile. The derelict remains of BnL's operations can be seen all around.

BnL Shipping

BnL Gas Stations

43

Flashback
The Captain is delighted to see EVE and places a memory chip on her head so that he can see what Earth looks like. As they look back through her memories, EVE can also see how WALL•E cared for her when she was in sleep mode.

Power Struggle
Auto is not impressed with the new, energized Captain. He reveals that BnL had given up on cleaning Earth a long time ago and ordered him to keep the *Axiom* in space forever.

After their romantic interlude in space, WALL•E and EVE return to the *Axiom*, determined to give the plant to the Captain. The Captain is a changed man since their last meeting—he has been excitedly researching Earth and can't wait to return there. Slowly but surely the other humans on the *Axiom* are also starting to sit up and take notice for the first time.

RED ALERT!

Important Mission
After Auto reveals the truth, he orders GO-4 to dump the plant down the trash chute. Fortunately WALL•E is on his way up the chute and arrives with the plant.

WALL•E can't bear to be parted from EVE!

Broken Hero
Auto and GO-4 reveal themselves to be truly unfriendly! First, GO-4 freezes EVE, and then Auto sends a surge of electricity through WALL•E and imprisons the Captain.

To the Rescue!
When EVE heads up the trash chute to see the Captain, she tells WALL•E to wait for her. However, he soon gets impatient and heads after EVE.

45

BACK HOME

Teamwork
While M-O saves EVE and WALL•E from being sucked into space, the Captain defeats Auto, by switching him off!

With Auto and GO-4 on a major sabotage mission, it seems that humans will never get back to Earth. However, WALL•E and EVE might be a little battered, but they are not finished yet! Thanks to some help from the reject-bots, the Captain, and the humans, Operation Recolonize is back on and it's time for the *Axiom* to set a course for Earth.

As a last resort, EVE holds WALL•E's hand. It works! Something stirs in WALL•E's memory and he calls out her name.

Her Hero
EVE finally realizes that she loves WALL•E, but she fears it is too late—his adventures have left WALL•E badly injured and in need of urgent repairs.

EVE is heartbroken when WALL•E can't remember her.

Saving WALL•E

Back on Earth, EVE uses spare parts in WALL•E's trailer to repair her special robot. Although this brings WALL•E back to life, he seems to have lost his memory and just wants to go back to cubing trash.

Faithful Friend

WALL•E's loyal Cockroach pal has been waiting patiently for him to return to Earth!

Happy Ever After?

As the humans take their first steps on Earth for seven hundred years, WALL•E and EVE share a tender moment. Together they watch the first sunset of a new era on Earth.

LONDON, NEW YORK, MUNICH,
MELBOURNE, AND DELHI

Art Editor Lynne Moulding
Senior Editor Catherine Saunders
Editor Victoria Taylor
Brand Manager Lisa Lanzarini
Publishing Manager Simon Beecroft
Category Publisher Alex Allan
Production Editor Siu Chan
Print Production Amy Bennett

First published in the United States in 2008 by
DK Publishing
375 Hudson Street
New York, New York 10014

08 09 10 11 12 10 9 8 7 6 5 4 3 2 1
WD170—04/08

Page design © 2008 Dorling Kindersley Limited
WALL•E Copyright © 2008 Disney Enterprises, Inc. and Pixar

Published in Great Britain by
Dorling Kindersley Limited.

DK books are available at special discounts when
purchased in bulk for sales promotions, premiums,
fund-raising, or educational use. For details, contact:

DK Publishing Special Markets
375 Hudson Street, New York, New York 10014
SpecialSales@dk.com

ISBN: 978-0-7566-3840-5

Reproduction by Media Development and Printing Ltd., UK
Printed and bound by Lake Book Manufacturing, Inc., USA

ACKNOWLEDGMENTS

Dorling Kindersley would like to thank:
Leeann Alameda, Mary Beech, Kelly Bonbright,
Kathleen Chanover, Ed Chen, Aidan Cleeland,
Lindsey Collins, Ralph Eggleston, Cherie Hammond,
Gillian Libbert,Holly Lloyd, Leigh Anna MacFadden,
Jim Morris, Desiree Mourad, Burt Peng, Jim Reardon,
Jay Shuster Andrew Stanton, Clay Welch,
and Timothy Zohr at Pixar Animation Studios.
Graham Barnard, Laura Hitchcock, Victoria Saxon,
and Chuck Wilson at Disney Publishing.

Discover more at
www.dk.com